Dear Parent:
Your child's love of reading starts here!

Every child learns to read in a different way and at his or her own speed. Some go back and forth between reading levels and read favorite books again and again. Others read through each level in order. You can help your young reader improve and become more confident by encouraging his or her own interests and abilities. From books your child reads with you to the first books he or she reads alone, there are I Can Read Books for every stage of reading:

SHARED READING
Basic language, word repetition, and whimsical illustrations, ideal for sharing with your emergent reader

BEGINNING READING
Short sentences, familiar words, and simple concepts for children eager to read on their own

READING WITH HELP
Engaging stories, longer sentences, and language play for developing readers

READING ALONE
Complex plots, challenging vocabulary, and high-interest topics for the independent reader

ADVANCED READING
Short paragraphs, chapters, and exciting themes for the perfect bridge to chapter books

I Can Read Books have introduced children to the joy of reading since 1957. Featuring award-winning authors and illustrators and a fabulous cast of beloved characters, I Can Read Books set the standard for beginning readers.

A lifetime of discovery begins with the magical words "I Can Read!"

Visit www.icanread.com for information
on enriching your child's reading experience.

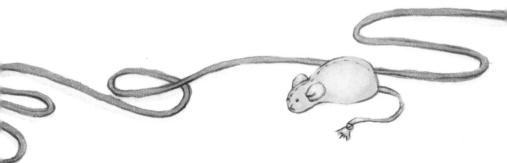

In memory of our cat Dickens
—L.M.S.

To Rob and Cyndi
—S.K.H.

HarperCollins®, 🐾®, and I Can Read Book® are trademarks of HarperCollins Publishers.

Library of Congress Cataloging-in-Publication Data
Schaefer, Lola M., date Mittens / story by Lola M. Schaefer ; pictures by Susan Kathleen Hartung.— 1st ed.
    p.   cm. — (My first I can read book)
    Summary: Nick helps Mittens the kitten adjust to life in a new home.
    ISBN-13: 978-0-06-054659-5 (trade bdg.) ISBN-10: 0-06-054659-X (trade bdg.)
    ISBN-13: 978-0-06-054660-1 (lib. bdg.) ISBN-10: 0-06-054660-3 (lib. bdg.)
    ISBN-13: 978-0-06-054661-8 (pbk.) ISBN-10: 0-06-054661-1 (pbk.)
    [1. Cats—Fiction. 2. Animals—Infancy—Fiction.] I. Hartung, Susan Kathleen, ill. II. Title. III. Series.
PZ7.S33233Mit 2006
[E]—dc22   2005019485

❖

Mittens

story by **Lola M. Schaefer**

pictures by **Susan Kathleen Hartung**

HarperCollinsPublishers

Nick has a new kitten.

His name is Mittens.

"Mittens, this is
your new home," says Nick.

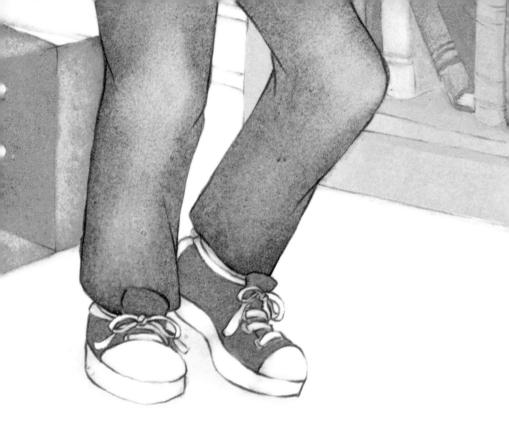

Mittens looks around.

Everything is new and big!

Mittens is scared.

Mittens wants a hiding place.
He wants a small place
just for him.

Zoom!

Mittens runs out of the room.

Zoom!

Mittens runs behind the T.V.

It is too loud.

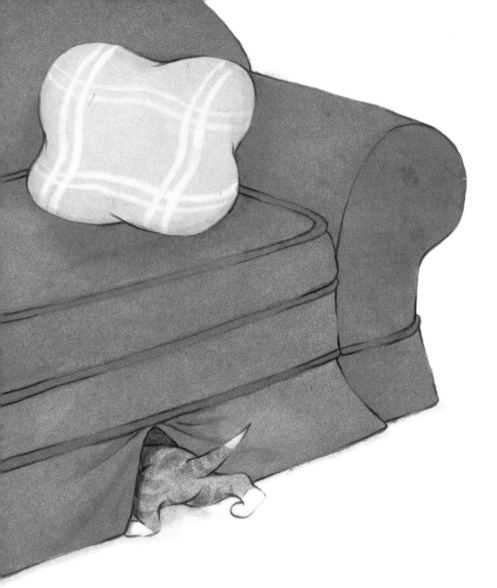

Zoom!

Mittens runs under the sofa.

It is too dark.

Zoom!

Mittens runs down the hall
and under a bed.

This is it!

Mittens has a hiding place.

14

He has a small place
just for him.

But everything is still new.

Mittens is still scared!

Mittens cries, "Meow!"

"Mittens, where are you?"
calls Nick.

"Meow! Meow! Meow!"

"There you are.
Don't cry, Mittens,"
says Nick.

19

Nick lies down.

"You are safe now," says Nick.

"I will take care of you."

Mittens moves toward Nick.
"I will be your friend,"
says Nick.

Mittens comes closer.

Nick waits.

Mittens curls up next to Nick.
"Welcome home, Mittens,"
says Nick.

Purrrrrr.

25